To Katrina, Benjamin, and Nancy Diener, with lo:
from Steve, LuAnn, Chrystal, & Bonnie Ramer

Patsy Scarry's

BIG BEDTIME STORYBOOK

by Patsy Scarry
illustrated by Cyndy Szekeres

Random House New York

For Fiona

Some of the stories in this volume were originally published in *Little Richard*
and *Little Richard and Prickles* by American Heritage Press.

Library of Congress Cataloging in Publication Data:
Scarry, Patsy. Patsy Scarry's Big bedtime storybook.
SUMMARY: Sixteen short stories about Little Richard, a rabbit,
and his adventures with his other animal friends in the woods.
1. Children's stories, American.   [1. Animals—Fiction]
I. Szekeres, Cyndy.   II. Title.   III. Title: Big bedtime storybook.
PZ7.S326Pa   1980   [E]   79-5450
ISBN: 0-394-83268-X (trade); 0-394-93268-4 (lib. bdg.)

Manufactured in the United States of America   4 5 6 7 8 9 0

Contents

Mother's Helper   9

Tracking   12

The Surprise   15

Be Sure to Bring It Home   19

Pirates   22

The Big Hike   25

What a Clever Rabbit!   29

Guests for the Night   32

Pockets   35

Baby-Sitting   38

The Birthday Present   42

The Message-Sender   46

The Saturday Surprise   51

Being Birds   57

First Snow   61

Here Comes Daddy!   66

Mother's Helper

Deep in the woods is a very small house. Flowers bloom in the windows. And everyone calls it Little Richard's house, because he is the fat little rabbit who lives there. He lives there with his mother and father.

One day, Little Richard hurried into the kitchen of that small house.

He sniffed and he smiled. Mother Rabbit was beating cookie batter in a bowl.

"Oh Mommy, you're making cookies. I will help you," said Little Richard. "I will put the raisins into the bowl." Because he was such a small rabbit, he had to climb up on a stool to reach the box of raisins.

He reached and wobbled. Ooops! He knocked the raisins down. The box bumped on his head and then spilled on the floor.

"Oooh! I wanted to help," wailed Little Richard.

"That's all right. There are some raisins left," said Mother Rabbit, shaking them into the bowl.

Little Richard watched his mother roll the cookie dough flat with a rolling pin.

"I will help you cut the cookies and put them into the pan," said Little Richard.

And while Mother Rabbit cut the round cookies with her cutter, Little Richard cut out star-shaped cookies with his cutter. It was fun.

But when he tried to put the cookie dough into the pan, it stuck inside the cutter. He shook it. And the dough landed on the floor!

He tried cutting another cookie. And *it* landed on the floor.

"Oooh! I wanted to help!" said Little Richard.

"You will help," said Mother Rabbit. She quickly cut out the cookies and shook them onto the cookie sheet. Now they were ready to bake.

"I will help you put them in the oven," said Little Richard.

"Oh no. The oven is too hot," said Mother. And she put them in the oven herself.

"In just a few minutes you can really help," said Mother Rabbit, as she swept up the floor.

The cookies were browning in the oven. Little Richard sniffed. He smelled the sugar and raisins and butter and cinnamon.

Then he watched his mother take the cookie pan out of the oven. She set it on the table to cool.

"*Now* you can help me, Little Richard," said Mother Rabbit. She put some warm cookies onto a plate and said, "You can taste the cookies for me."

And that's what Little Richard did!

He tasted one cookie, and it tasted so good that he said, "Yum!" Then he reached for another, and another.

"They taste delicious!" said Little Richard. "You are the best mother in the whole world!"

"And you are the best helper in the whole world," said Mother Rabbit with a smile. "You are very, very good at tasting cookies!"

Tracking

"Little Richard, aren't you going outside to play?" asked Father Rabbit.

"It's too muddy to play," said Little Richard.

"Then you could go tracking. Muddy days are just right for tracking," said Father Rabbit.

"What is tracking?" asked Little Richard.

"Why, it's looking for paw tracks in the ground. Here, I'll draw you a tracking chart," said Father Rabbit.

He got out his pencil and a piece of paper, and he made a chart for Little Richard.

Beside each paw print he drew the face that it belonged to.

There were bear tracks.

And rabbit tracks.

Raccoon tracks.

And bird tracks.

And duck tracks.

Little Richard was very pleased with his chart.

"I think I'll go tracking right now and see what I can find, Daddy," he said.

"Good luck," called Father Rabbit from the door. "But don't bring home any elephants!"

Little Richard put his nose close to the ground and looked for tracks in the damp earth. Right away he found a little bug.

"I am a tracker. Where are your tracks?" asked Little Richard.

"I haven't got any tracks. I'm too small," said the bug.

Then he found some funny web-shaped tracks, and he followed them all the way to the pond.

When he looked at his chart, it told him that they were duck tracks. And sure enough, a duck, paddling in the pond, called to him, "Quack! Quack!"

Little Richard went searching for more tracks in the earth, and

at last he came to a very strange track. It was big and round and not like a paw print at all.

"What is it?" wondered Little Richard.

It wasn't a duck track or a rabbit track. And it was bigger than a bear track. Maybe it was an elephant track! Little Richard thought perhaps he should go home, quickly.

Then, looking up, he saw a friendly face.

"Hello. You're an owl, aren't you?" asked Little Richard. "Why don't you make tracks like an owl?"

"Because today I'm a whumper," said the friendly bird, whose name was Owley.

"Oh," said Little Richard. Then he asked as politely as possible, "What's a whumper?"

The bird smiled.

"A whumper is something that stands in a sack. It jumps up and comes down with a WHUMP! Like this!"

Then the whumper whumped and whumped until he'd whumped right out of sight, leaving big round tracks behind him.

"Just wait till I tell Daddy!" said Little Richard. And he ran all the way home to tell Father Rabbit how he'd tracked down a real live whumper!

The Surprise

"Will you come for a walk in the woods with me, Mommy?" asked Little Richard.

Mother Rabbit buttoned his jacket and said, "I'd like to, Little Richard. But I have things to do before lunch."

"But where can I walk to?" asked Little Richard. "What will I do all alone?"

"You can look for something," said Mother Rabbit. "Look for a nice surprise and bring it home for lunch."

So Little Richard set out to look for a nice surprise.

He walked until his nose told him to stop. And where he stopped there was a fine big bush of strawberries!

His mother loved strawberries. And so did Little Richard. Strawberries would be good for lunch. So he picked all that he could find.

But where did they go? Into his pockets?

No. They all went into Little Richard's mouth, that's where! Because young rabbits just love strawberries!

So Little Richard walked on through the woods, looking for a nice surprise to bring home for lunch.

He looked into a hollow log and into shiny puddles, but he didn't find any surprises. Until, sitting in the sunshine, he saw a pretty yellow flower! He knew his mother loved flowers. So Little Richard picked it.

He held the flower tightly in his paw. And he was just about to hurry home when he saw that it was wilting. How sad!

Its strong green stem was bending over, and its petals drooped sadly.

"Oh, you poor flower. I shouldn't have picked you," said Little Richard.

He poked a hole in the earth and put the flower into it so it would feel at home. Then he hurried along, looking for a surprise to bring home for lunch.

He stopped. On top of a rock, in the shade, was a bit of late spring ice. Now that would be good to bring home, thought Little Richard. His mother could put the ice in her lemonade.

He found a stone, and he chipped that bit of ice off the rock. Pleased with himself, he put it into his pocket. But he had walked only a few steps before he felt something wet and dripping. Oh! The ice chip had melted.

Little Richard would have to go home without a surprise.

Then he heard a strange, grumbling noise. It was coming from a large bush that seemed to be shaking its leaves.

Out of the bush jumped a porcupine.

He looked at Little Richard and shook his head crossly.

"Nothing is ripe enough to eat," said the porcupine. "The skunk cabbage is late this spring. Everything is late. I spend all my time looking for something ripe enough to eat. What are you looking for?" he asked.

"I'm looking for a surprise," said Little Richard. "My mother told me to bring home a nice surprise for lunch."

"Oh," said the porcupine thoughtfully. Then he waddled over to Little Richard, with a big, friendly smile, and said, "I know of a nice surprise to bring home for lunch."

And he whispered into Little Richard's ear.

Well, Mother Rabbit was delighted when she opened the door. For Little Richard's new friend was the surprise he had brought home for lunch!

"This is Prickles," said Little Richard.

It was lucky that his mother had made a huge pot of cabbage soup. It was Prickles' favorite.

He and Little Richard became best friends right away.

And Mrs. Rabbit said that Prickles was the very nicest surprise Little Richard could have brought home for lunch.

Be Sure to Bring It Home

Little Richard and Prickles were on their way to buy groceries.

Mrs. Rabbit held out her umbrella to them.

"Oh Mommy, do we have to take that?" asked Little Richard.

"Yes, dear. And be sure to bring it home," said his mother.

As they walked to the store, Little Richard played leapfrog with the umbrella.

"Say, that looks like fun," said Prickles. "It *is* fun," he said, laughing, as he jumped over the handle, too.

Creak! went the umbrella.

"Uh-oh, the handle is bent," said Prickles.

"We'd better stop jumping over it," said Little Richard. "I promised we'd bring it home."

Prickles held the big umbrella safely off the ground. Then he started a new game. He marched, swinging the umbrella up and down like a drum major's baton. Little Richard marched smartly behind him.

"Ooompah pah! Ooompah pah!" they sang.

They marched under a tree. Just for fun, Prickles gave a big jump and hooked the handle over a limb. The umbrella opened, and he hopped inside it.

CRACK!

The handle broke off. The umbrella and Prickles landed on the grass with a thump.

"Now how will we get the handle down?" asked Little Richard.

"We can't," said Prickles. "But never mind. We've got the most important part."

They tried to close the umbrella, but it was no use.

"And now we have to drag it all the way to the store and back home again," Little Richard groaned.

"But we promised your mother we'd bring it home," said Prickles.

By now the umbrella was a nuisance to carry. A wind blew up, and the two friends held on to it fiercely.

20

Splash! Splash! Fat raindrops began to soak their feet.

"It's lucky your mother made us take the umbrella," said Prickles.

But just then, the wind tried to pull it from their grasp. They hung on.

RIIIIIIIIIP!!

With a wrenching, ripping sound the wind turned all the wire spokes of the umbrella inside out!

Little Richard and Prickles had never seen anything like it!

"You run home, Prickles," called Little Richard. "I'll take the umbrella home to Mother. What's left of it."

"But what about the groceries?" asked Prickles.

"The bag would get wet and break," said Little Richard.

And they both waved good-by and hurried home through the rain.

As he dashed inside his house, Little Richard held up the bent, broken, blown inside-out umbrella.

"Look, Mommy, I brought it home!" he cried.

Poor Mother Rabbit. She had no groceries and no umbrella. She should have been angry. But when she looked at her little rabbit proudly holding the smashed umbrella, she burst out laughing.

"Yes, you did keep your promise!" she said.

And she gave him a big hug.

Pirates

Little Richard's father was going to read the newspaper in the garden hammock. But he found it filled with pirates.

"Yo ho ho!" cried Little Richard and his friends, rocking the hammock wildly.

"Now why aren't you pirates out hunting for buried treasure?" asked Father Rabbit.

"We don't know where to look, Mr. Rabbit," said Prickles.

Then they all began shouting again.

Father disappeared. But in a little while he was back at the pirate ship.

"Haven't any of you pirates noticed that strange paper pinned to the tree?" he asked.

"Hey look, it's a map!" cried Owley.

The pirates crowded around the map. It had pictures of bushes and a stream and tall grass. And under a tree a box was buried.

"It must be buried treasure," said Little Richard. "Look, the trail starts right over there. Let's go!"

Father flung himself into the hammock and rocked happily as the pirates set off to hunt for treasure.

"The map says to go around the berry bushes," said Little Richard.

They did that. Then they crossed the five big stones that bridged the stream and crawled through a hollow log. Nothing in there! Then they came to three big trees.

"According to this map, the box is buried under the third tree," whispered Little Richard.

"Why are you whispering?" asked Raccoon.

"Because if it *is* buried treasure, something may be guarding it," whispered Little Richard.

"Something?" whispered Owley, nervously.

"Let's go home," said Prickles.

"I hope it's a box filled with gold coins so we can buy candy," said Raccoon.

The pirates crept toward the tree.

"There's a hole in the bottom of this tree," whispered Little Richard.

"Ah, I feel something," he cried. And out of the hole he pulled a box.

"I hope it's not p-p-poison," stuttered Owley.

"Go ahead and open it," said Raccoon.

Little Richard put the box on the ground and poked at the lid with a stick.

"Hurrraaay!" cheered the pirates. For inside the box were lollipops and licorice pipes and funny wax teeth. What a treasure!

They were so excited they rushed back to the hammock, where Little Richard's father had fallen asleep.

"Mr. Rabbit, guess what? We really *did* find treasure!" cried the pirates.

"No!" said Father Rabbit, amazed.

"Yes, here it is, and you may have some," said Prickles.

Father helped himself to a red lollipop.

Then all the pirates sat on the grass, eating their treasure and smiling.

"That was exciting," said Little Richard. "Daddy, do you think we'll find treasure *every* time we're pirates?"

"Not *every* time," said Father. "But maybe once in a while." And he put the newspaper over his face to hide his smile.

The Big Hike

Little Richard and Prickles were packing for a hike. It was to be a long, long hike. So there were lots of things to carry.

Little Richard had his knapsack filled with tin plates and a fishing rod, a flashlight for the dark, and his popgun to frighten scary things away.

Prickles was carrying a sheet for a tent, some sticks to hold the tent up with, and the sweater his mother had forced him to bring.

"My goodness, you have so much to carry. Where can I put the lemonade and brownies?" asked Mother Rabbit.

"Oh Mommy, we don't have room for a picnic," said Little Richard.

"We'll hunt for something to eat, like real campers do," said Prickles.

Mother Rabbit smiled and somehow squeezed the thermos and brownies into her son's sack. Then she waved good-by to the hikers.

"We'll be home in a week. Maybe two," called Little Richard. Then up, up the meadow they climbed.

They had so much to carry that, after a few minutes, the meadow seemed as high as a mountain.

"We must have climbed two miles already," panted Little Richard.

"Oh, twice as high!" said Prickles. He was so hot and tired that he flung himself on the grass.

"Well, we've reached the top of the meadow," said Little Richard, sitting down with a bump.

"Ouch!" he cried as he sat on the thermos his mother had put in his sack. The hikers were very happy to find the lemonade and brownies.

They had a nice picnic as they watched a big, black cloud spread its shadow across the grass.

Raindrops began to splash as the hikers set up their tent. It wasn't easy. The tent wanted to lie down, the way all sheets do. So the hikers climbed under it, poking it up with sticks. And down came the rain, in big, wet drops.

"Brrr!" shivered Little Richard and Prickles.

When at last the rain stopped, the sun cast long, scary shadows across the meadow. The hikers were wet and hungry.

"Doesn't a week of camping seem a bit long? Won't your mother be lonesome?" asked Prickles.

"Y-yes," said Little Richard. His teeth chattered with cold.

"I can see the lights gleaming down there in your house," said Prickles.

"Oh, let's go home now," said Little Richard.

"Well, only if you really want to," said Prickles happily. "But now we have to climb all the way down!"

Just then, Little Richard made a lucky discovery. He found a big clump of skunk cabbage. He broke off the two biggest leaves, and he gave one to Prickles. The other one he sat on.

Then, with his knapsack on his back, he slid on his cabbage leaf, bump, bump, bump, down the meadow!

Prickles followed, bumpety-bump, behind him!

27

Oh, the Rabbits' cottage looked so bright and cozy when Father opened the door. He was very surprised.

"Why, we didn't expect you home for a week!" he said.

A fine stew simmered on the stove.

"I set two extra places at the table, just in case of company," said Mother Rabbit.

The two hikers climbed into dry pajamas and sat at the table, happy to be home. They both ate second helpings.

Prickles yawned and said, "As my mother always says, it's nice to be away but it's nice to come home, too."

Little Richard yawned as well. And soon Father Rabbit carried two sleeping hikers off to Little Richard's room, to bed.

What a Clever Rabbit!

Father Rabbit had so many hats!

He had a hat for rainy days. And a hat for fishing. And a hat for sunny days. And a hat for Sunday best. And his favorite hat. He had so many hats that they lay all over the house. They were always getting sat on!

On the bedroom wall were two big hooks to hang things on. But no one ever did.

Sometimes Mother Rabbit would put all the hats away neatly in the bedroom closet.

Then Father Rabbit would pull them all out of the closet, trying to find his favorite hat. And all of his hats would land on the bedroom floor, where they stayed until Mother picked them up again.

One night, when it was very late and very dark, the wind blew hard, and the rain dashed against the windows of Little Richard's house. Then there was a terrible CRACK! outside the window.

In the dark bedroom Father Rabbit tripped over his rainy-day hat and his fishing hat and his hat for sunny days. But when he got to the window, it was so dark outside that he couldn't see what had gone CRACK!

Then he tripped over all his hats again and went back to bed.

In the morning they all went outdoors to find that the CRACK! had been made by an old dead tree limb that had fallen down in the storm.

"It looks sad lying there," said Little Richard.

That afternoon, while Mother Rabbit was at the market buying food for supper, Prickles came to visit. He found Little Richard very busy in the bedroom. Little Richard was making a surprise, and he told Prickles that he could help.

The surprise was finished before Mother Rabbit came home. Then Little Richard waited all tiptoey for Father Rabbit to come home for supper. And at last he did.

He flung his favorite hat on the couch, and he seemed to be limping a bit.

"I banged my paw when I tripped over my hats last night," he said.

Then he went into the bedroom. Little Richard hugged himself with excitement. He waited, and waited. Then he smiled as he heard Father Rabbit cry out: "Oooooh! What a lovely surprise!"

His father was smiling proudly as he called Mother Rabbit into the bedroom to show her the surprise. They both said, "Oh, how beautiful!"

For over the two big hooks on the wall Little Richard had hung that old dead tree limb.

And on each little branch he had put one of his father's hats, so that they sat up there in a neat and tidy way.

"It's such a handy hat rack!" said Father Rabbit.

"And it's very pretty, too!" said Mother.

They were both so proud of Little Richard that he felt like quite the cleverest little rabbit in all the world!

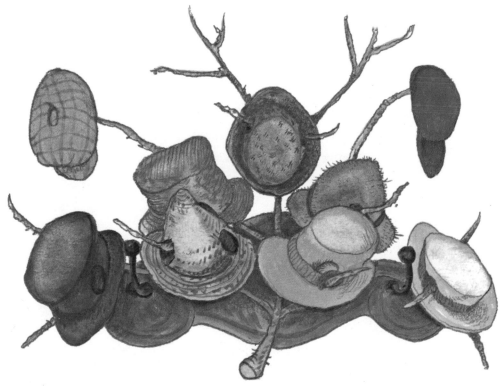

Guests for the Night

Prickles and Owley were staying overnight at Little Richard's house.

They had had a wonderful evening, and now it was time for them to go to bed.

"Good night! Sleep tight!" they called as they climbed upstairs.

"They've been so good," said Mother Rabbit.

But just at that moment, right over her head, there was a loud THUMP!

The house shook. And the pictures went crooked on the wall.

"What happened?" cried Father, and he raced up the stairs.

Little Richard and his friends were jumping on the bed.

"Stop!" shouted Father Rabbit. The bed collapsed with a terrible crash.

"Oh no!" he groaned.

Little Richard looked at the sagging bedposts and said, "Excuse us, Daddy. We forgot to wash our faces."

"Well, hurry up," said Father, as he tried to fix the bed. Little Richard and his friends made a quick getaway.

Soon howls and splashes came from the bathroom.

Downstairs, Mrs. Rabbit looked at the ceiling. Then at the wall. She blinked her eyes and said, "Father, is that water dripping down the wall?"

"Good grief. It is!" He jumped up and shouted, "What are you children doing up there?"

"Just washing our faces, sir," called Prickles.

Owley slipped on a piece of soap and fell halfway down the stairs. Then they all raced into the bedroom to sleep. Well, almost.

Little Richard had put a sheet over his head. He was a ghost. And he was so scary that his friends squealed with fright. They were hiding in the closet.

Every time they opened the door, the ghost was there.

Oh, how they squealed!

"If I have to come up there, you'll be sorry!" called Father Rabbit. The noise stopped.

Thump! Thump! Thump! They jumped into bed.

"Little Richard is tickling me!" giggled Prickles.

"Little Richa-a-a-arrrd!" called his father in a warning voice.

"Now he's pushing me out of bed!" howled Prickles.

THUMP!

"I'm not pushing him anymore, Daddy," called Little Richard.

"When are you children going to sleep?" roared Father Rabbit.

There was a long silence. Then a voice called softly, "We're asleep now, Mr. Rabbit."

The house was silent. Mother listened nervously.

"It's just too quiet," said Father. "I'm going up to see what's going on."

Together they tiptoed up the stairs. The room was a shambles! But there were three little heads on the pillow, sound asleep.

"Just look at those little angels," whispered Mother Rabbit.

"*Angels?*" said Father.

Later on, Father Rabbit smiled at Mother over the newspaper. "They really are good children," he said.

34

Pockets

Little Richard was wearing his very first suit. It was a beautiful shade of blue, and it had many pockets.

"You look handsome in your new suit," said Mother Rabbit.

"And very grown-up," said Father.

But Little Richard felt shy.

"Everyone will stare at me. They will ask me what the pockets are for," he said.

"Tell them that pockets are to put things into," said Father Rabbit. And he dropped a shiny penny into the very top pocket.

Right away the suit didn't feel quite so new.

Little Richard put his paws into his side pockets and said, "Thank you, Daddy. I think I'll go for a walk."

The first friend he met was Prickles.

"Hello, Little Richard. I like your new suit. What are all the pockets for?" asked Prickles.

"They are to put things into," said Little Richard.

Prickles stared at Little Richard's new suit. Then he said, "You can have this pine cone to put into your pocket. I just found it."

It was a very big pine cone, and it took a bit of pushing, but it made a nice lump in Little Richard's pocket.

"Thank you, Prickles. Now my suit doesn't feel so new," said Little Richard.

"Let's show your new suit to Owley," said Prickles.

And off they went to his house. Owley said that the new suit was very nice. He especially liked the pockets. Then he offered his friends some fudge that his mother had just made.

"Take as much as you want," he said.

Mmmm, it was warm and sticky. Little Richard took one piece for eating and stuffed two other pieces into his pocket.

Then they wandered down to the stream where they met
Raccoon, who was fishing. He admired Little Richard's new suit.

"We're trying to fill up his pockets," said Prickles.

Raccoon dug into his bucket and said, "Would you like this
nice little fish to put into your pocket, Little Richard? It's
dead."

And of course Little Richard was delighted to fill up his very
last pocket.

Father Rabbit was working in the garden. And when he saw
Little Richard's new suit with the pockets bulging, he dropped his
shovel. Then he laughed and laughed.

"Your suit doesn't look so new, Little Richard," he said.

"That's because we filled up all the pockets," said Prickles. "I'll
bet his mother will be surprised when she sees him!"

And she was.

37

Baby-Sitting

Little Richard and Prickles were walking down the lane near Mrs. Hedgehog's house. The noise was terrible!

"Your babies are crying, Mrs. Hedgehog," said Little Richard.

"They've climbed out of their cradle," said Prickles.

"Yes, they're crying because it's nap time," sighed Mrs. Hedgehog. She pulled a dry sock off the clothesline and called to her babies, "Climb into your cradle, dears. Mother will rock you to sleep."

Prickles and Little Richard chased the babies and helped them into their cradle.

"They just won't sleep unless they're rocked," said Mother Hedgehog. "And they must have a nap before we go to the store."

Prickles and Little Richard helped to rock the cradle, and right away the babies stopped crying.

"Why don't you go to the store now, Mrs. Hedgehog? Prickles and I will baby-sit for you," said Little Richard.

"Oh, my goodness. That would be wonderful!" said Mrs. Hedgehog. She picked up her shopping bag and hurried down the lane. Then she looked back at her babies rocking quietly in their cradle.

"Good by, darlings!" she called. Right away, the little hedgehogs sat up.

"Now, go to sleep," said Little Richard, pushing at the cradle.

Prickles pushed, too, and soon the cradle was rocking wildly. The little hedgehogs loved it.

"Your mother promised you'd sleep if you were rocked," said Prickles.

The cradle was rocking dangerously now. Then, whoops! It turned right over, and the little hedgehogs tumbled out onto the grass. They ran behind the tree where the clothesline hung and climbed into the laundry basket.

"Now they'll never take their nap," said Prickles.

"Yes, they will," said Little Richard. He climbed into the cradle and called, "Look at me, babies, I'm going to sleep in your bed."

Right away the baby hedgehogs scrambled back into the cradle. They bounced on top of Little Richard. Oh, what fun!

CRACK!

The cradle broke in two.

When they saw their broken cradle, they all began to cry at once.

"Oooooh!"

Little Richard tried making funny faces, but he only frightened them. Prickles clowned, and they began to scream. The baby-sitters were beginning to need a nap, too.

"Maybe we could make a hammock out of a sheet to rock them in," said Prickles. He dug into the laundry basket. No sheets.

Then Little Richard looked at the clothesline and saw Mr. Hedgehog's overalls hanging there, stiffly dry and covered with pockets.

"Now there is a good cradle," he said, grinning. And it was.

Oh, how Mrs. Hedgehog laughed when she saw her baby-
sitters! They both sat under the tree pulling the legs of Mr.
Hedgehog's overalls. Back and forth they rocked, and the pockets
were filled with little hedgehogs—all fast asleep.

"What good baby-sitters you are. Why, you can sit for me
every day if you'd like to," said Mrs. Hedgehog happily.

"Um, thank you, Mrs. Hedgehog," called Prickles and Little
Richard. They hurried down the lane. Then they broke into a
run. For Mr. Hedgehog's overalls had stopped rocking, and those
busy babies were waking up again.

The Birthday Present

Father Rabbit had an ugly old pair of boots that he liked. And he always left them wherever he stepped out of them. Sometimes he even left them on the living room carpet, all muddy and wet. Mother Rabbit was not fond of those boots.

One morning when Prickles came over to Little Richard's house, he tripped over one of the boots, which was lying on the front lawn. He kicked it along for a while, because he was thinking hard.

"Little Richard, today is my mother's birthday. Can you think of a nice present I can give her?" he asked.

"Maybe we could make her something," said Little Richard. "What does she like the best?"

"She likes flowers. And she likes antiques. You know, old things," said Prickles.

They both looked at Mother Rabbit's garden of pansies nodding in the sunshine.

"I know my mother won't mind if we dig up a few flowers," said Little Richard.

"But what could we put them into?" asked Prickles. "We have to find something old, like an old tree stump. Or . . ." and Prickles smiled. "What about this old boot? We could plant the flowers in this boot!"

"Oh, I don't know. I think it belongs to my father," said Little Richard.

"What? That? Why he wouldn't wear anything like that! See how the toe curls up? And it has no laces. Nobody would wear *that!*" said Prickles.

"Maybe you're right," said Little Richard. "Let's plant some pansies in this old boot right now. I'll get the trowel."

The two friends dug up some of Mrs. Rabbit's flowers and gently planted them in the old boot. Then they sprinkled them with water.

And they tied a beautiful pink ribbon around the boot.

It certainly was an unusual birthday present. They were very excited. They ran right over to Prickles' house to give it to his mother.

Father Rabbit came home and kicked off his good shoes. Now where had he left his comfy boots? He looked under the bed and on the living room carpet. Then he hobbled out to the kitchen, with one old boot on, and said, "Mother, have you seen one of my work boots lying around? It's missing."

"No, dear, I haven't," said Mother.

"Oh, now I remember. I kicked it off in the garden last night because I had a pebble in it," said Father Rabbit. And he clumped outdoors to look for his other boot.

"Mommy! Daddy! Come quickly!" called Little Richard. "Mrs. Porcupine wants you to come and see the birthday present Prickles and I gave her. She loves it!"

44

Mother and Father Rabbit followed Little Richard to Prickles'
house.

"Isn't that beautiful?" asked Mrs. Porcupine. She pointed to
her kitchen windowsill, where Father Rabbit's beloved old boot
was sitting, filled with Mother Rabbit's pansies.

"Why, it's lovely," said Mother Rabbit, smiling.

Father looked down at his one lonely boot and frowned. Then
he managed a big grin and said, "It's so pretty, Mrs. Porcupine,
I don't know what to say!"

Then they all sat down at the picnic table for a piece of
birthday cake.

45

The Message-Sender

Little Richard called out of his window, "Hello, Raccoon, can you hear me?"

No answer. So Little Richard ran across the lawn to the hollow tree where Raccoon lived.

Raccoon was leaning out of the window, pulling dry laundry off the clothesline.

"Raccoon, I've been calling you from my window. Didn't you hear me?" asked Little Richard.

"No," said Raccoon. "I have this job to do for my mother, and I just wasn't listening."

Little Richard stood under the clothesline and folded the laundry neatly in a pile.

"I think we should have a message-sender," he said.

"A what?" asked Raccoon, pulling on the clothesline.

"A way to send notes to each other," said Little Richard.

Raccoon sent a pillowcase sailing down on his friend's head.

"We could have a secret whistle," he said.

"No. That's not secret enough," said Little Richard. "We'd still have to shout our messages."

Raccoon unhooked the last piece of laundry from the clothesline. Then he slid down the pole of the clothesline and said, "It should be a message-sender that is hitched from your window to mine . . . with a little bell on it."

"Yes," said Little Richard. "It should be something that we can pull back and forth like . . . like a CLOTHESLINE!"

"Yes," said Little Richard. "A clothesline would be just right!"

They both laughed. Because right above them hung the perfect message-sender. A pulley clothesline!

"Is it long enough to reach between the windows?" asked Little Richard.

"If we add some string to it," said Raccoon. And that's just what they did. In a little while the clothesline was stretched between Little Richard's window and Raccoon's. They pulled on the line, and it moved smoothly back and forth.

"Oh this is going to be fun!" cried Raccoon.

He printed a note and pinned it to the line with a clothespin. Then he tugged on the line. The message bobbed along to Little Richard's window.

"Got it!" cried Little Richard. And he squealed with pleasure as he opened his message.

"Now I'll send one to you!" he called.

They had a wonderful time making up funny messages to send

to each other on the clothesline. They were laughing so loudly that they didn't hear Mrs. Raccoon come home.

She smiled when she saw the laundry neatly folded on a rock. And when she saw the messages passing in midair she cried, "What a clever invention!"

"Yes, we don't have to shout anymore, Mrs. Raccoon," shouted Little Richard.

"That's wonderful," said Mrs. Raccoon. "Where did you find such a long line?"

"We didn't exactly find it. We borrowed it," said Little Richard.

"You did?" she asked. "Well, whoever let you have her clothesline to play with is a very nice person. I wouldn't let anyone use mine."

Mrs. Raccoon wandered around the tree to gaze up at her own clothesline.

"Oh dear. It's gone!" she said. She placed her paws on her hips. She frowned. She pursed her mouth. And she looked puzzled.

Little Richard and Raccoon were worried.

Then she burst out laughing.

"You shouldn't have taken it without asking," she said. But just to show that she didn't mind too much, she took a sack of cookies out of her grocery bag, pinned it to the message-sender, and watched it move to Little Richard's window.

A message came back.

"It's for you, Mommy," cried Raccoon.

She opened the paper and read aloud, "Thank you. You are so nice."

Then, with a smile, she tucked the message into her pocket.

"You can keep the clothesline as long as you want," she said. "Well, at least until next washday."

The Saturday Surprise

The four little hedgehogs who lived down the lane had the flu. It was sad. They couldn't leave their house. And no one could visit them until they were well.

Mrs. Hedgehog met Little Richard and Prickles at the store. She asked them if they would come and wave up at the window.

"That would cheer them up," she said.

So that is just what Little Richard and Prickles did. They waved. And the hedgehogs waved back. They seemed a little bit cheered up.

On the way home, Little Richard had an idea for entertaining them. He told his idea to Prickles, who said, "That's a wonderful idea. But I'd be afraid to do some of those things."

"No, Prickles, we'll practice," said Little Richard.

Raccoon and Owley wanted to join them in the plan, when they heard about it.

"When will we do it?" asked Owley.

"On Saturday," said Little Richard. "But first we must practice."

"I'm afraid," said Prickles.

"No, you're not!" said Little Richard.

From inside Little Richard's room his mother could hear bumps and thumps. And when she knocked on the door, it opened just a bit.

"We're practicing our surprise for Saturday, Mommy," said Little Richard.

"What is it?" asked Mother.

Little Richard told her about his plan.

"It's a secret. Don't tell," said Little Richard.

"I won't," promised Mother.

"We have to practice now," said Little Richard. And he gently closed the door.

Inside the room Prickles was complaining.

"I can't do it. I'm afraid of heights!"

But his friends shouted encouragement.

"Be brave, Prickles!"

"Climb up the ladder a little higher. Higher!"

There was a thump! Prickles fell on the floor for the fifth time.

Meanwhile, Owley raided the trunks in his family's attic. He took funny old hats, furs, beads, and jackets from his house. His mother called from the window, "Where are you taking those things?"

"It's a secret, Mom. We'll bring them back," called Owley.

All week long they practiced. Then on Saturday morning they marched to the Hedgehogs' yard. Little Richard banged on a drum. And the four little hedgehogs rushed to the window.

"What's going to happen?" they wondered, very excited.

Little Richard hung a sheet from the fence so that it made a tent.

In a few minutes he leaped out of the tent wearing a tall silk hat and a red jacket that hung down in folds around him. He pounded his drum.

"Welcome to the circus!" he called up to the Hedgehogs' window.
Everyone in the woods heard the noise and came running to see
the fun.

Little Richard announced that the first performer would be
Fearless Raccoon, the lion tamer.

Raccoon ran out of the tent holding a stick with a string tied to it.
He snapped it smartly over his head, and Prickles sprang into the
yard.

He wore a paper ruffle around his neck, and he snarled as he
lunged about.

Little Richard placed a cardboard box on the grass, then a higher
one beside it. Raccoon, the lion tamer, cracked his whip, and
Prickles jumped onto the first box, howling fiercely. Raccoon
cracked his whip again. Prickles jumped and landed on the higher
box, wobbling.

When Raccoon turned to bow, the wicked lion leaped down and
chased him into the tent, growling as if he were going to eat him up.

54

The little hedgehogs loved it! They clapped and cheered. Imagine having their very own circus!

The next act was Owley, the Strong Man. He slowly lifted a pair of barbells. A sign on the barbells said they weighed two thousand pounds each! With much groaning and pulling he lifted them right over his head. Then he danced around on the grass. Everybody cheered!

Next came the tumblers, turning cartwheels.

Then Prickles appeared wearing a little skirt and holding a parasol. Little Richard helped Prickles climb onto a big beach ball. He held Prickles' paw as Prickles walked on top of it. This was a very difficult trick. Prickles was just becoming brave when the parasol caught on the branch of a tree. The ball rolled away and poor Prickles was left dangling!

Everybody clapped. And Little Richard rescued him.

Last of all came four funny clowns. They bumped into each other and did stunts. Then they balanced on top of each other in a pyramid.

"More! More!" called the little hedgehogs.

Little Richard held up his paws and said, "The circus is over for today. Shall we come back tomorrow?"

"Oh, please do!" called the hedgehogs from the window.

So Little Richard and his friends put on a circus every day until the hedgehogs were all better. Everyone agreed that Little Richard's circus was the best medicine anyone could think of.

Being Birds

ne day Little Richard and Prickles decided
to be birds.

The nest was Mother Rabbit's laundry basket. They tied a
long rope to the handles and put in lots of cookies. It was cozy.

"What are you doing?" asked Mother.

"We are being birds," said Little Richard.

"Birds?" asked Father. "Don't birds live in trees?"

"Yes, Daddy. Would you pull us up into the tree, please?" asked
Little Richard.

Father Rabbit flung the long rope over a high limb of the tree.
Then he pulled, and up, up went the basket.

"Higher, Daddy, higher! It's wonderful up here!" called Little
Richard.

"I think we are high enough," wailed Prickles.

"Yes, Father, that's high enough," said Mother Rabbit. "They'll
have to stay up there until we come back from shopping."

"I've tied a big knot so the basket won't fall," said Father Rabbit.
And off they went to shop.

"Tweet! Tweet!" chirped Little Richard and Prickles.

It was nice being up in a nest. At least Little Richard thought so. The leaves rustled softly, and the great sky felt close.

"Stand up with me and look at the view, Prickles," said Little Richard.

"No thank you," cried Prickles. "You're swinging our nest!"

Little Richard sat down.

"I think I'm getting airsick," said Prickles, nervously.

"Here, eat a cookie. You'll feel better," said Little Richard. The cookies tasted so good they ate them all. Then the birds settled back and tweeted to each other for a while.

"I wonder what birds do for fun?" said Little Richard, feeling restless.

"They fly places," said Prickles. "I wish we could."

The wind blew up. It made the basket sway.

"I feel dizzy," moaned Prickles.
"I don't want to be a bird anymore."
They tried calling for help.
"Hello down there! Can somebody
let us down?"
"Hellllp!"
But nobody came.
Prickles began to cry.
"Don't worry, Prickles. I'll slide down
the rope and get you down, somehow," said Little Richard bravely.
Oh, it was a very long way to the ground.
Little Richard was trembling. But down, down to the bottom of
the rope he slid, all the way to the ground.
Poor Prickles. Little Richard could hear him crying, all alone, up
there. How could he get him down?
To lower the nest gently he had to tie something heavy to the
rope. He looked around for a stone, or a big piece of wood. There
was nothing.
Little Richard untied the rope and quickly wound it around his
own middle. Then he began to climb up the tree. Higher and
higher. He was feeling a little bit scared. But down came the nest,
very gently, with Prickles in it.
"Hi!" said Little Richard as they passed in midair.
"Where are you going?" shrieked Prickles. "Up?"

"It was the only way," said Little Richard. "I'll tie the rope around a branch and slide down."

With a little bump Prickles landed on the ground. He wished Little Richard were with him.

So did Little Richard. The rope was too tight around him. He untied it. But before he could loop it over a branch, it slipped out of his paws! Oh no! He watched it fall. Now he was all alone in the tree with no rope to help him get down!

The wind blew hard. The tree swayed dangerously. Little Richard tweeted to keep his courage up. But he didn't feel like a bird.

Prickles shouted some brave words from the ground and then left.

Little Richard waited. Now the sun was going down. Has everyone forgotten me? he wondered.

Then all of a sudden he saw a big ladder at the foot of the tree. It was his father coming to save him!

"Tweet tweet!" called Little Richard, bravely.

"Tweet tweet!" sang his father. They tweeted all sorts of little tunes until he was safe in his father's arms at last.

60

First Snow

Little Richard ran from his room calling, "Mommy! Daddy! It snowed last night!"

Everyone hurried to the window to see the snow heaped like thick white icing on the meadows and trees. Then Little Richard hurried to get dressed. He hurried through breakfast. He hurried out into the snow and danced in it and flung it over himself. Then he began to make a big snowball.

"I'm going to make a snowman in my own front yard," he said.

Prickles came running through the snow, calling, "Little Richard, will you help me make a snowman in my yard?"

"If you'll help me make mine first," said Little Richard.

Raccoon came to help. He wanted a snowman in his yard, too.

"I want a big, big snowman. As big as Daddy," said Little Richard.

Mother Rabbit called from the window, "Roll the snowball down the hill. It will gather snow on its way."

"But then it won't be in my own yard," said Little Richard.

"That's all right. You can see it from the window," said Mother.

So everybody pushed the big snowball. It began to roll slowly, then faster and faster, until it rolled away from them.

They had to chase it down into the meadow. And they all were excited to see how fat it had grown.

Owley hurried from his house, very pleased, because now the snowball was almost under his tree.

They worked all day. And at last the huge snowman stood, round and smiling, at the bottom of the meadow. He had an old hat on his head, buttons of coal, and a long carrot for a nose.

Father Rabbit came down the hill, and he said it was the handsomest snowman he had ever seen.

"Now all of you hurry to our house, because Mother has made cocoa and brownies," he said.

They raced up the hill, looking back at the snowman.

"Daddy, aren't you coming, too?" asked Little Richard.

But the wind blew his question away.

Inside Little Richard's house, wet mittens and caps dripped by

the fire. They all sipped cocoa and talked about their snowman.

"I don't really care if he isn't in my own yard," said Little Richard. "After all, we made him together."

"And we can see him from our houses tonight," said Owley.

"Only if the moon shines brightly," said Raccoon.

They were just finishing the brownies when a snowball hit the window. Little Richard ran to see who it was.

"It's Daddy," said Little Richard. Then he called, "Oh, come and look! Hurry!"

Everyone ran to the window. They sighed and said, "Isn't our snowman beautiful!"

For down in the meadow, Father Rabbit had planted a ring of tall candles in the snow. They gleamed all around the snowman so that he glistened in the dusk for everyone to see.

"Now *all* of us can see him from our houses tonight," whispered Raccoon.

And everybody smiled happily.

Here Comes Daddy!

Every night, after his bath, Little Richard climbs into his bed, and Mother Rabbit reads him a bedtime story.

Then she gives him a good-night kiss. And she says, "Daddy will bring you a glass of water."

Little Richard always laughs. He scrunches way down under the covers, and curls himself into a little round ball.

No one would ever guess that a rabbit was in bed at all!

Then he tries to be ever so, ever so quiet. Because here comes Daddy!

Every night Daddy says the very same thing.

He says, "Did somebody call for a glass of water?"

Then he looks all around Little Richard's room.

"Why, I thought there was somebody here!" he says.

And he puts the water down on the table.

"I just know I heard somebody call," says Daddy. "Perhaps there's somebody in the closet."

Daddy looks.

"No. Nobody's in the closet."

"Maybe there's somebody under the bed."
Daddy looks.

"No. There's nobody under the bed."

Then Father Rabbit sits down on the bed. And the small bed squeaks and bends so that somebody hiding inside the bed giggles!

"Now I KNOW I heard somebody laugh. But where can he be?" asks Father Rabbit, very puzzled.

Daddy leans way back on the bed and almost squashes the little round ball under the covers. Something squeaks.

"Well, what is this lump doing here in the bed, I wonder?" asks Daddy.

He pats it with his paw. And the round ball giggles.

He tickles it. And the round ball squeals.

Then Father Rabbit says, "What is down there inside my Little Richard's bed?"

And suddenly the covers come off and Little Richard sits up, laughing.

"It's me! It's Little Richard!"

Why, Daddy is so surprised and pleased to see him that he gives him a big rabbit hug.

And he says, "Good night, my Little Richard."

Then he turns out the light and tiptoes out the door.

"Good night, Daddy. Good night, Mommy," calls Little Richard.

"Good night! Good night!"

"Sleep tight!"